P9-DUT-320
3 3020 01115 3789
IR

outpost zero™

CREATED BY SEAN KELLEY McKEEVER & ALEXANDRE TEFENKGI

Westminster Public Library
3705 W. 112th Avenue
Westminster, CO 80031
www.westminsterlibrary.org

SKYBOUND

FOR SKYBOUND ENTERTAINMENT ROBERT KIRKMAN Chairman DAVID ALPERT CEO SEAN MACKIEWICZ SVP, Editor-in-Chief SHAWN KIRKHAM SVP, Business Development BRIAN HUNTINGTON VP, Online Content SHAUNA WYNNE Publicity Director ANDRES JUAREZ Art Director JON MOISAN Editor ARIELLE BASICH Associate Editor KATE CAUDILL Assistant Editor CARINA TAYLOR Production Artist PAUL SHIN Business Development Manager JOHNNY O'DELL Social Media Manager SALLY JACKA Skybound Retailer Relations DAN PETERSEN Sr. Director of Operations & Events Foreign Rights Inquiries ag@sequentialrights.com Other Licensing Inquiries contact@skybound.com WWW.SKYBOUND.COM

image

IMAGE COMICS, INC. ROBERT KIRKMAN Chief Operating Officer ERIK LARSEN Chief Financial Officer TODD MCFARLANE President MARC SILVESTRI Chief Executive Officer JIM VALENTINO Vice President ERIC STEPHENSON Publisher / Chief Creative Officer COREY HART Director of Sales JEFF BOISON Director of Publishing Planning & Book Trade Sales CHRIS ROSS Director of Digital Sales JEFF STANG Director of Specialty Sales KAT SALAZAR Director of PR & Marketing DREW GILL Art Director HEATHER DOORNINK Production Manager NICOLE LAPALME Controller WWW.IMAGECOMICS.COM

FOLLOW IT DOWN

SEAN KELLEY McKEEVER
CREATOR/WRITER

ALEXANDRE TEFENKGI
CREATOR/ARTIST

JEAN-FRANCOIS BEAULIEU
COLORIST

ARIANA MAHER
LETTERER

ARIELLE BASICH
EDITOR

ANDRES JUAREZ
LOGO DESIGN

CARINA TAYLOR
PRODUCTION DESIGN

OUTPOST ZERO VOLUME 2. FIRST PRINTING. May 2019. Published by Image Comics, Inc. Office of publication: 2701 NW Vaughn St., Ste. 780, Portland, OR 97210. Copyright © 2019 Skybound, LLC. Originally published in single magazine form as OUTPOST ZERO #5-9. OUTPOST ZERO™ (including all prominent characters featured herein), its logo and all character likenesses are trademarks of Skybound, LLC, unless otherwise noted. Image Comics® and its logos are registered trademarks and copyrights of Image Comics, Inc. All rights reserved. No part of this publication may be reproduced or transmitted in any form or by any means (except for short excerpts for review purposes) without the express written permission of Image Comics, Inc. All names, characters, events and locales in this publication are entirely fictional. Any resemblance to actual persons (living or dead), events or places, without satiric intent, is coincidental. Printed in the U.S.A. For information regarding the CPSIA on this printed material call: 203-595-3636.
ISBN: 978-1-5343-1216-6

volume two

I WAS WATCHING THE EXCAVATION VIDFEED, YOU KNOW.
YOU SHOULD BE, TOO, UH...
...LYSS, YOU SAID IT WAS?

WHY WOULD I BE WATCHING?
IT'S IMPORTANT. THEY GOT TO REMOVE ALL THAT ICE OVER OUR HEADS.
RIGHT, BUT...WILL MY WATCHING IT CHANGE THE OUTCOME IN ANY WAY?

NOT THE POINT. IT MATTERS, WHAT HAPPENS AROUND US MATTERS--
OH.

IS THIS RIGHT? TWO RECREATION LOANERS ON THE SAME DAY?
THAT DOESN'T REALLY HAPPEN.

I KNOW!
I'VE BEEN COUNTING THE DAYS FOREVER.
THIS IS MY SINGULARITY.

TWO REC LOANERS, ONE PERSON, ONE DAY, FLAW IN THE SYSTEM IS WHAT IT--
WELL, HERE WE'VE GOT THE EAR PLAYERS...

WHAT'S IN THEM?

MUSIC. HOMEWORLD ERA, SAYS THE METADATA. IT'S WHATEVER WAS LOADED WHEN GENSHIP OH-EIGHT CRASH-LANDED HERE.
NO ONE KNOWS HOW TO CHANGE THE LINEUP, SO DON'T ASK FOR--
IT'S FINE.

NOW THESE...

...WITH THESE YOU NEED TO BE VERY CAREFUL.
IT'S THE ONLY PAIR LIKE THIS WE GOT LEFT, AND WE CANNOT FABRICATE NEW ONES.
THEY AREN'T LIKE THE INDUSTRIAL TYPE. STAY BELOW THE TREE LINE OR YOU COULD BE IN REAL TROUBLE.

GOT ANY QUESTIONS?
JUST ONE.
HOW JEALOUS ARE YOU RIGHT NOW?

BE SAFE OUT THERE, LYSS.

WOOOOOWOO!
I was lost at sea when I saw you

I swore

I'd never seen nothing like that
like that

CAN YOU BELIEVE IT, DEAN? THERE'S A CRISIS.
THAT'S LYSS. SERVICES TEAM INTERN.
SERVICES? SHE DOESN'T CARE ABOUT ANYTHING, DOES SHE?

Most beautiful trees of green
and a shore
with grains of the finest of fair sands
fair sands
PUT SOME CLOTHES ON!
though you were so far away
and the roiling waters beckoned me to stay
I just had to gain access to
the island of you...

LOOKS LIKE...
...UH...
...SOME FLUCTUATION HERE, BUT WE'RE STILL WITHIN DENSITY PARAMETERS FOR TUNNELING.
WHAT DO YOU SAY, JANN? FULL SPEED AHEAD?
SLOWLY AHEAD, PLEASE, DENIS...
BURY US, WE BURY EVERYONE.
NOW CAN WE TALK, SAM?
INSTEAD OF WATCHING THIS PLAY OUT?

ALEA...
YOU GAVE ME MY PROJECTOR BACK, AND I HELD UP MY END.
I TOLD YOU HOW STEVEN WAS ABLE TO GET OUT INTO THE FROST.
IT'S OVER NOW.
I MEAN, I DON'T SEE WHAT ELSE...
I'VE BEEN TRYING TO MAKE SENSE OF IT. WHY THIS WAS THE LAST THING STEVEN SAID BEFORE HE STEPPED OUT OF THE AIRLOCK AND...
BEFORE HE WENT AWAY.
FOLLOW IT DOWN
FOLLOW IT
THERE IS NO MAKING SENSE OF IT.
MAYBE WE JUST DIDN'T REALLY KNOW HIM. SOME PEOPLE JUST DON'T SHOW SIGNS...
SPEAK FOR YOURSELF.
YOUR PROJECTOR, SAM. THE RECORDING OF THAT GIRL.
LINDA? WHAT ABOUT HER?
THE GENSHIP ANCESTRY PROJECT-- THE G.A.P.
YOU SAID IT'S ALL DOWN IN THE STEM SOMEWHERE-- A WHOLE LIBRARY OF RECORDINGS FROM OUR PAST.
AND...?
FOLLOW IT D
IT DOWN
DOWN IN THE STEM.
DOWN.

SO YOU THINK HE--
STEVEN DIDN'T ***KNOW*** I HAD THE PROJECTOR. YOU'RE THE ONLY ONE--
UNLESS ***YOU*** TOLD SOMEONE.

RIGHT. YOU DIDN'T FIND OUT 'TIL LATER. HE COULDN'T HAVE KNOWN.

BUT HE KNEW ***SOMETHING*** WE DIDN'T. HE SAID ***WE*** HAVE TO SAVE THEM.
US.
YOU AND ME.
IF SOMETHING MAKES EVEN A LITTLE SENSE, WE ***HAVE*** TO LOOK INTO IT.

I WAS RIGHT. SHOULD ***NEVER*** HAVE TOLD YOU WHAT HE SAID.
WHAT?
EVEN IF HE KNEW ABOUT THE ***G.A.P.*** SOMEHOW, AND HE KNEW ***I*** KNEW ABOUT IT, WHICH IS ***INSANE***--

--THE CONNECTION WAS DELIBERATELY ***SEVERED.*** I MEANT WHAT I SAID--***NO ONE*** WANTS THIS STUFF RECOVERED.

SO YOU'VE ***SEEN*** THIS SUPPOSED ACT OF SABOTAGE.
I FOUND THE RELAY MY PROJECTOR CONNECTS WITH, YEAH.
SO... WHERE'S THIS RELAY?

HEY!
ALEA--
IF I'M RIGHT ABOUT THIS--
WE DON'T KNOW WHO CUT THE CONNECTION OR WHY OR HOW MANY ARE INVOLVED--
WE DON'T EVEN KNOW IF THE G.A.P. IS IN ANY WAY FUNCTIONAL. WE'D BE IN DEEP TROUBLE OVER NOTHING.
HEY. PLEASE.
YOU'RE RIGHT. WE DON'T KNOW. BUT, SAM...
...WOULDN'T YOU LIKE TO KNOW?
SAM?
IT'S...
IT'S IN ONE OF THE SERVICE BUNKERS.
LOCKED.
I DON'T HAVE ACCESS ANYMORE.
THAT'S OKAY.

island of you

island of
AAA!

YOU ALMOST HIT ME!
SERVICES TEAM'S BEEN CALLED IN.
GERALD-- IT'S MY DAY OFF!
NO EXCEPTIONS-- CRIMINALS, INTERNS, EVERYONE.
WE REST TODAY, WE DIE.

ALL THAT ICE IS STRESSING THE DOME, SO WE'RE SETTING OFF THE STEAM BANKS.
WHAT'S THAT GONNA DO?

THE HEAT'LL MAKE A LIQUID BARRIER, THEY SAY.
DISTRIBUTE THE WEIGHT, EASE THE BURDEN.
HIT THE BUNKERS. YOU GOT THIRTY-SIX TO FORTY-ONE.
AND DON'T RUSH IT.
DO THAT, THE STEAM BANKS'LL BLOW.

your icy winds and your waves
made it so
I only wanted to go back
go back
still I pressed ahead as creatures
below
37
38
36
39
40
41
they circled me for their attack
for their snack--
CLIC
OKAY. GET THIS OVER WITH FAST.
CRRE
JUST NOT TOO FAST.

NNH. COME ON...
STUBBORN...
CRRR
THERE WE--
NOTHING.
NOTHING BACK THERE.
CRRR
HURRY, HURRY.
NO NO NO! SLOW DOWN, SLOW DOWN.
CRRR

4
NOW, WHO'S--
THERE'S NO ONE DOWN HERE, IT'S ALL IN YOUR HEAD.
FIVE MORE.
ONLY FIVE MORE.

HA!
YOU DIDN'T GET ME, STEAM RELEASE BUNKER!
CLIC
it filled my heart with fear
all your threats and torments made it very clear
there would be no one passing through

the island
of you...
island of
you...

island of
you...

I HAVE TO GO BACK, STRETCH MY LEGS, GET OUT...
JUST A FEW MORE HOURS, JOSH. WE NEED YOU.
I CAN'T.
I CAN'T.
YOU'RE OKAY. JUST BREATHE.

WHEN I WAS DOWN THERE? UNDER THE OUTPOST? IT WAS WEIRD.
I FELT THERE WAS, LIKE, SOMEONE ELSE.
BUT THERE WASN'T.

IT'S CREEPY IN GENERAL DOWN IN THOSE THINGS.
EVERYTHING ECHOES, THE COLD CUTS THROUGH YOUR CLOTHES...
YEAH. AND I WAS WEARING THIS.

SO, LYSS...
SAM AND I... WE'RE DOING AN EXPERIMENT. I FIGURED YOU'D BE COOL WITH GETTING US ACCESS TO THE COMMUNICATIONS RELAY BUNKER--
NO.

THAT'S IT? JUST "NO"?
I'M NOT MY BEST SELF LATELY, AND IT--

I'M TRYING, ALEA.
WITH ALL THE STUFF GOING ON, I'M TRYING, BUT I FEEL LIKE AT ANY SECOND I'M GONNA--
DENIS!

LOOK OUT!
AH!
GNAAAAAA!
ZAP
OPEN THE AIRLOCK! OPEN IT NOW!
IT'S JOSH!
NO.
NO NO NO NO...
CAN ANYONE HEAR ME?!
I CAN'T--
ARE YOU OKAY?
I...

crashed hard upon your beach and
I knew
that you were going to strike me
to spike me
I braced myself to be snuffed out
when you
swore there could be nothing like me
like me
--TOO HIGH, MOMMY. IT'S TOO HIGH!

THAT'S TOO BAD, BECAUSE I WANT YOU TO SEE.

WHY ARE THEY DOING ANOTHER WALL?
BECAUSE WE'RE NOT SURE THE STORM WALL CAN PROTECT US ON ITS OWN.
EXTRA WALL WILL PROTECT US?
WHAT DO YOU THINK?
I DON'T KNOW. I HOPE IT CAN.

I DO, TOO. BUT OUR DOME WAS SUPPOSED TO BE UNBREAKABLE.
THEN THAT STORM CELL CAME AND BROKE THE UNBREAKABLE DOME AND A WHOLE LOT OF PEOPLE WENT AWAY.
THEY DIED.

THAT'S RIGHT. THEY DIED.
HONEY, WE'RE NEVER SAFE. NOT EVER.
BUT DON'T YOU DARE LET THAT SCARE YOU, OKAY?
INSTEAD...

...LET IT FREE YOU.
the hazards you had made
they only served to keep yourself afraid
KRIZZZ
so that no one ever knew

SNAP
the island of you...

KNOCK
KNOCK
HEY.
THIS PLAN OF YOURS AND SAM'S?
I'M IN.

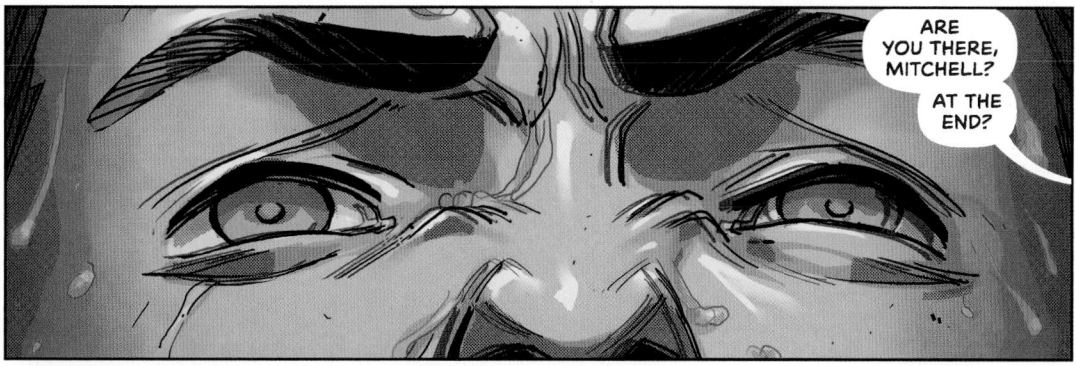
ARE YOU THERE, MITCHELL?
AT THE END?

YOU DON'T HAVE MUCH TIME LEFT.

EVERYTHING THAT'S LED UP TO NOW IS FOR NOTHING IF YOUR HEAD JAMS UP ON YOU.
YOU CAN'T LET OTHER STUFF IN.

TO WIN, YOU HAVE TO SEE THE END.
DO YOU SEE IT?

OF COURSE.

REMEMBER, YOU CAN'T BE HERE TO SEE IT.
YOU CAN'T BE ANYWHERE BUT THERE.
THERE, IN THE MOMENT, FULL CLARITY, YOUR OPPONENT LYING BEFORE YOU.
FORGET YOUR PROBLEMS.
SURVIVAL DEMANDS YOU PUT YOUR LIFE ASIDE AND--
ZWIIISH
I TOLD YOU...
I SEE IT.

NO, ALEA. NO WAY.

OUR DEAL WAS--
FORGET THE DEAL, THIS ISN'T--
THIS IS ***POST-DEAL,*** SAM.

LYSS IS MY CLOSEST FRIEND. I TRUST HER COMPLETELY.

EVERY PERSON WE TELL ABOUT THE ***GENSHIP ANCESTRY PROJECT*** INCREASES THE CHANCE OF THE ***WRONG*** PEOPLE KNOWING WE KNOW.

AND THE MORE PEOPLE KNOW I WAS THE LAST TO SEE STEVEN AND...
AND IF THEY KNOW I WAS IN THE AIRLOCK...
I'M LATE! I KNOW. SORRY.

MY PARENTS ***INSIST*** ON EXCAVATION WATCH BEFORE BED--TO "KEEP US APPRECIATIVE"--SO I COULDN'T SNEAK OUT.
OKAY! SO, ARE WE READY FOR ADVENTURE AND EXCITEMENT?

THIS... DOES NOT EXCITE.
HOW ARE YOU EVEN SUPPOSED TO KNOW WHAT ANYTHING'S FOR?
HARD TO BELIEVE ALL OF THIS WAS USED ONCE. WE'RE PROBABLY GETTING BY WITH HARDLY ANY OF IT.
NO WAY TO REALLY TELL.
WHAT ARE YOU AFTER DOWN HERE?
ANYTHING THAT LOOKS LIKE IT MIGHT LEAD INTO THE STEM.
WE JUST KIND OF WANNA SEE WHAT'S DOWN THERE--IF WE CAN.
WE'RE ALMOST BETTER OFF NOT KNOWING, THOUGH, RIGHT?
SOME THINGS JUST GET ADDED TO THE LIST OF THINGS WE CAN'T DO ANYTHING ABOUT.
I MEAN, WE CAN'T EVEN CHANGE THE MUSIC ON THOSE LITTLE EAR PLAYERS, SO THIS--
UH, LYSS, YOU TOLD ME WE CAN'T IGNORE THE UNKNOWN BECAUSE IT'S EVERYWHERE. AND ANYWAY--
--WE'RE DOING IT BECAUSE STEVEN ASKED US TO.

DID YOU JUST--
I DID. IT'S DONE.

STEVEN? I... DON'T UNDER-STAND...
HE THOUGHT SAM AND I COULD FIND SOMETHING DOWN IN THE STEM TO HELP THE OUTPOST. HE SAID SO BEFORE HE...
WE'RE NOT SURE WHAT OR WHY OR HOW, BUT HE ***WANTED*** US TO TRY.

WHY DIDN'T YOU JUST TELL ME STEVEN WAS BEHIND THIS?
OF COURSE I'M GONNA HELP...
YOU'RE RIGHT. WE ***SHOULD*** HAVE SAID SO FROM THE START. BUT SAM DOESN'T REALLY KNOW US YET.

HEY, THAT'S... YOU KNOW, YOU ***ARE*** GONNA FIND OUT YOU CAN TRUST US. SERIOUS.

THIS IS A GOOD THING, SAM. TAKE IT.

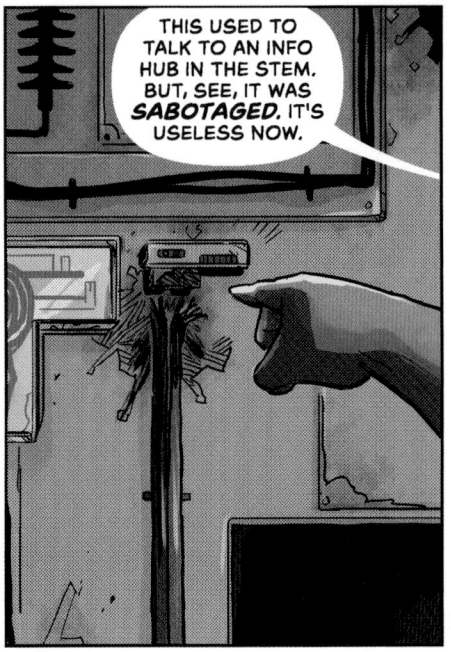
THIS USED TO TALK TO AN INFO HUB IN THE STEM. BUT, SEE, IT WAS SABOTAGED. IT'S USELESS NOW.

HOW DO YOU KNOW ALL--
YOU CAN'T TELL ANYBODY, LYSS. EVERYTHING I'M TELLING YOU, SHOWING YOU?
NOT YOUR FAMILY, YOUR FRIENDS--

TAKE IT EASY, SAM. SHE UNDERSTANDS.
LET'S TRY TAKING OFF THE BASE COVER.

WE'D HAVE TO TAKE THE WHOLE THING APART.
WHICH COULD BREAK SOMETHING IMPORTANT.
MIGHT, YEAH.

JUST WONDERING... DOES IT MATTER WHERE YOU GET TO THE STEM FROM?

TWO MORE DEGREES AND--

NO POWER?!
DID WE LOSE THEM?
KIDS! WHERE ARE YOU?!
NOT AGAIN!

EVERYTHING'S ALRIGHT! IT'S JUST ANOTHER BROWNOUT!
POWER WILL RETURN SHORTLY!

HEY. HEY, ARE YOU--?

WHAT?
IT'S YOU. YOUR DEBUT'S COMING UP.
YEAH. I'M AWARE.

THERE HASN'T BEEN A FIGHT SINCE THE CELL.
EVERYONE'S SO--WELL, YOU KNOW.
JUST WANTED TO SAY THANK YOU. WE NEED IT.

KNOW HOW MANY FIGHTERS LIVE TO SEE THEIR TWENTIETH BIRTHDAY, MITCHELL?
OR KNOW IT'S THEIR TWENTIETH?
YOU'RE ONE OF THE COMPLAINERS ALL OF A SUDDEN?
WHAT, BECAUSE I'M FIGHTING?
I'LL BE SO GOOD I'LL NEVER GET HIT ONCE. YOU'LL SEE.
I DON'T PLAN TO SIT THERE AND SEE YOU--
JUST BECAUSE YOU THINK THIS IS WHAT YOU WANT FROM LIFE--
NO, YOU'RE RIGHT.
WHAT I REALLY WANT DEEP DOWN IS FARMING TEAM.
AFTER ALL, IT'S BEEN SUCH A BOON TO OUR FAMILY.
AND LOOK AT WHAT AN EXCITING GUY IT MADE YOU.

HAVE TO BE UP EARLY.
TAKE MINE TO YOUR SISTER. HASN'T BEEN OUT OF HER ROOM SINCE SHE GOT HOME.
GOT YOUR FAVORITE. FARMER LEM'S LEFTOVER SURPRISE.
MITCHELL.
HEY, MITCHELL.
WHEN DID YOU START *TAKING* THIS LATE?
SO GOOD TO SEE YOU.
MY OTHER HALF.

I NEED TO GO FOR A RUN.
NOOO, STAY.
STAY AND TALK.
WE NEVER TALK LIKE WE USED TO.
TAKE SOME TIME...TAKE SOME TIME WITH ME.
IF YOU'D TELL ME WHO'S PROVIDING, I CAN GO SEE ABOUT IT.
YOU'D LOVE IT. YOU CAN TALK ABOUT ANYTHING WHEN YOU'RE ON.
IT DOESN'T MATTER...
YOU COULD EVEN SAY SOMETHING LIKE, "MOM WOULD RATHER KILL HERSELF THAN RAISE US."
SEE...?
WASN'T DIFFICULT AT ALL...

IT'S LIKE NOTHING'S DOWN THERE.
DARKNESS FOR DAYS.
SEE?
THESE CREEPY SERVICE BUNKERS ARE CONNECTED TO THE STEM.
NOT MUCH OF AN OPEN GAP. GOOD THING, SAFETY WISE...
HOW FAR DO YOU THINK IT GOES?
WAY FARTHER THAN I WOULDA THOUGHT...
WHAT ABOUT YOUR GRAVITY THING? THAT JUMP YOU DID WITH STEVEN?
WOULD THAT HELP?
GRAVITY THING?
NO, THAT WOULDN'T--
THE MATH'S OFF, ANYWAY. WHAT DO YOU THINK, SAM? CAN WE DO ANYTHING WITH THIS?
I'D-- WELL, I'D HAVE TO GET INTO THE SCRAP WAREHOUSE...WHICH I NO LONGER HAVE ACCESS TO.
SO YOU'RE GIVING UP.
I DIDN'T SAY THAT.

DO YOU TALK TO YOUR PARENTS AT ALL?
THEY CHECK IN WHEN THEY CAN. BASICALLY MAKING SURE I HAVEN'T STRANGLED ELLA...

I MEAN, KAREN'S UNMARRIED. MAYBE SHE THINKS IT'S HYPOCRITICAL TO PRESSURE ME. WHY? ARE ***YOUR*** PARENTS...?
YOU COULD MARRY MITCHELL. CALM HIM DOWN.
OH, THEY'VE STARTED. "THINK ABOUT WHO YOU'RE GOING TO ***MARRY,*** YOUNG WOMAN!"
THAT WOULD BE IMPRESSIVE...

THIS SOME KIND OF PRANK?!
HEY.
FIRST STEVEN, NOW YOU'RE GONNA INFECT MY FRIENDS? IS THAT WHAT YOU'RE DOING, SAM?
HEY.
WHAT'S WRONG WITH YOU?
ME?!
YOU'RE SPENDING TIME WITH THAT WEAK, LITTLE--
DID YOU NOT SEE HIM AFTER HIS PARENTS DIED?
MOST PATHETIC, SPINELESS THING EVER! HE'S GONNA BRING YOU DOWN!
WHAT? OH, I'M WRONG?
TELL ME I'M WRONG!
MITCHELL...

COME ON, SAM.
GOOD LUCK WITH YOUR FIGHT, MITCHELL. I HOPE IT DOES SOMETHING FOR YOU.
GOTTA BE KIDDING ME.
SERIOUSLY, LYSS. YOU KNOW HE'S NO GOOD...
I WISH I KNEW HOW TO HELP YOU.
HELP ME?
HELP ME WHAT?
I'M NOT THE ONE WHO--
I'M JUST TRYING...
...
YOU KNOW WHAT? I'VE GOT THINGS TO DO.
GO AND PLAY WITH YOUR FRIENDS.

SEE THE END.
IS THAT...?
HEY...YOU DON'T HAVE TO KNOCK...

I SEE IT EVERY DAY.
HOW THE WORLD WAS BEFORE I WALKED INTO THE KITCHEN.

HOW SHE WAS LYING THERE, NOT MOVING, STARING AT THE CEILING.
CHANGING EVERYTHING.

SHE LOOKED...IT WAS LIKE SOMEONE TRIED MAKING A COPY OF HER AND DIDN'T QUITE...
BUT IT WAS MOM.

MADDIE...

CAN I ASK YOU TO STOP TAKING? JUST LONG ENOUGH TO COME TO MY DEBUT?

MITCHELL. OF COURSE I WILL.
MY STRONGER HALF.
ALWAYS MY STRONGER HALF...

YOUR TIRELESS EFFORTS WITH THE SPECIAL JOINT EMERGENCY TEAM HAVE BEEN APPRECIATED BY ALL.

THANK YOU FOR YOUR SERVICE TO THE OUTPOST, JOSH. WE'RE LUCKY TO HAVE YOU.

THEY **NEED** THIS MORE THAN EVER.
A FRESH FACE. A FRESH WIN.
HOW ARE YOU GONNA DO IT?
SEE IT.

SEE WHAT?
SEE THE END.
THE MOMENT. MY OPPONENT LYING BEFORE ME.
BE THERE.
YOU GOT IT. NOW CLOSE YOUR EYES.
I WANT YOU TO TELL ME...

WHAT DO YOU SEE?

--HERE FOR HIS DEBUT, YOUR NEW CHALLENGER!

MITCHELL

FOURTEEN-YEAR-OLD MITCHELL HAS TRAINED AND ARRIVED IN HONOR OF YOU ALL!

LET HIM HEAR YOUR APPRECIATION!

NOW, THE CHALLENGER'S FIRST TEST OF WHAT WE HOPE WILL BE MANY TO COME...

...HERE'S ANTOINE!

FIFTEEN-YEAR-OLD ANTOINE HAS NOTCHED UP FIVE IMPRESSIVE WINS IN A ROW.
ASKED WHAT INSPIRES HIM TO KEEP FIGHTING, HE SAYS, "BECAUSE EVERY ONE OF US IS FIGHTING!"

NOW, WITHOUT FURTHER DELAY...

WHAT DID I TELL YOU?
WHAT DID I SAY?
VISUALIZE IT. SEE IT. FORGET THE REST.
AND WHAT DID YOU DO?
YOU DID IT, MITCHELL.
YOU WON.

THAT SHOULD BE PLENTY.
THERE WE GO.
THE HARD PART'S FINALLY OVER.

NOW FOR THE HARD PART.

EXPEDITION TO OUTPOST: WE'VE REACHED DAYLIGHT.

AND YOU THOUGHT IT WOULDN'T WORK...

I WAS *CONCERNED* IT WOULDN'T WORK.
THERE'S A DIFFERENCE.

CHIEF, SCAN OF YOUR TABLET LOOKS GOOD, AND I LOADED THE LATEST VIDCLIP COMPILATION.
THANKS, VIVIEN. ANYTHING UNUSUAL?
FOR SAM?
UNUSUAL'S ONE WAY TO PUT IT.

I THINK HE'S FINALLY MADE SOME *FRIENDS.*

BRINGING LYSS INTO THE FOLD--BE HONEST, SAM.
STILL ANNOYED, BUT...YEAH.
GOOD MOVE.

MUST BE NICE TO HAVE YOUR PARENTS HOME.
JUST A DAY OR TWO WHILE THEY GET READY FOR WHAT'S NEXT. I'LL BARELY SEE THEM, SO WHATEVER.
I MEAN, OF COURSE--ANY TIME WITH THEM, I'LL TAKE IT...

SO, DID YOU GET THE WAREHOUSE CODE FROM YOUR CH--
FROM KAREN?
SHE UPDATED HER TABLET'S PASSKEY. AND ASKING NICELY WON'T WORK.

OKAY, BUT...WE HAVE TO GET IN, RIGHT?
THERE HAS TO BE SOMETHING IN THE WAREHOUSE THAT CAN GET US AROUND THE BUNKER GRATE.
HOW ELSE CAN WE SEE IF THERE'S A WAY DOWN INTO THE STEM IF WE DON'T--
SAM...?

HEY, ALEA.
DO YOU KNOW WHERE TO FIND SOME ROPE?

YOU'RE GOING SOMEWHERE?
WHY? IS SOMETHING...?
NO, I JUST THOUGHT WE'D--
HOW'VE YOU BEEN?
I DUNNO. FINE.
I CAME UP WITH THIS IDEA-- LIKE, FOR A CLASS PROJECT. IT'S GONNA BE SO--
ANYWAY...
IS EVERYTHING OKAY? LIKE, WITH YOU?
YEAH. NO, IT'S--
YEAH. YEAH.
YOU GO AHEAD.
I'LL BE HOME FOR DINNER!
HAVE FUN.

HEY!
LYSS!

WHERE'RE YOU HEADING OFF TO?
MITCHELL.
HI.

YOU LOOK--
MY MOM'S REALLY GOOD AT HER JOB. IT'S LIKE YOU WERE BARELY IN A FIGHT.
SHE SAID YOU WERE REALLY SOMETHING...

I DIDN'T EXPECT YOU THERE, CONSIDERING. THANKS FOR ACKNOWLEDGING MY EXISTENCE, AT LEAST, UNLIKE ALEA.
I PROMISE I WON'T GET ALL--
I JUST-- I NEED YOU TO TELL ME ONE LITTLE THING...

WHAT'S GOING ON? WHAT ARE YOU GUYS *UP TO* WITH HIM? AM I NOT EVEN ALLOWED TO KNOW?
MITCHELL...

IT'S NOT FOR ME TO TELL.
YOU DO LOOK GOOD. I MEAN IT.

YOU SHOULD EAT MORE.
I TAKE UP TOO MANY RESOURCES. TOO MUCH OF PEOPLE'S TIME.
NOW, DOCTOR XI... AFTER SO MANY OF US TOOK UP YOUR TIME, IT'S ONLY FAIR.
SOON MY BODY WILL BE HARVESTED AND COMPOSTED AND I'LL BE A PROVIDER AGAIN. AND THAT'S THE LAST THING I'LL BE.
SIXTY-ONE YEARS. I CAN'T SAY I DIDN'T LIVE A LIFETIME.
A LIFE FILLED WITH EXPERIENCES, REALIZATIONS, FRIENDSHIPS, CHALLENGES.
CHOICES.
HOW'S YOUR BOY? HOW'S SAM?
HE'S ACTUALLY SPENDING TIME WITH OTHER KIDS, IF YOU CAN BELIEVE IT. I HARDLY CAN. TWO GIRLS.
SAW HIM TODAY, AND IT WAS LIKE HE WAS... LOOKING FORWARD TO THINGS. HAPPY.
AND YOU WOULDN'T WANT TO DO ANYTHING THAT MIGHT JEOPARDIZE THAT.

PLEASE DON'T.
YOU KNOW HOW SAM CAN BE...
HE'S SAD-- DON'T WANT TO MAKE HIM WORSE. NOW HE'S HAPPY-- WOULDN'T WANT TO RUIN THAT.
HE CAN'T BE DISTRACTED RIGHT NOW. HE'S INSULAR. HE'S DIFFICULT.

PART OF BEING A DOCTOR IS THAT I'LL TAKE A WHOLE LOT OF SECRETS WHEN I GO.
BUT WHAT YOU HAVE TO SAY TO SAM, THAT WON'T LEAVE WITH ME. OTHERS KNOW IT, TOO.

EACH NEW DAY BRINGS A CHANCE THAT SOMEONE ELSE WILL SAY SOMETHING TO HIM.
I CAN ONLY IMAGINE THE HUMILIATION YOUR SWEET BOY WOULD SUFFER, KNOWING YOU COULD HAVE TOLD HIM ALL THIS TIME BUT WOULDN'T.
THAT'S NOT FAIR. YOU DON'T KNOW.

OH, SURE I KNOW.
IT'S AN AWKWARD SUBJECT, AND YOU CAN RATIONALIZE THAT AN OMISSION ISN'T *TECHNICALLY* LYING.
BUT IF YOU WERE TO BROACH THE SUBJECT, SAM WILL HAVE QUESTIONS...

...AND THEN YOU'D HAVE TO DECIDE WHETHER YOU'RE GOING TO LIE TO HIM *OUTRIGHT.*

WHERE DID YOU FIND ALL THIS?
THERE WAS A FLOOR PANEL MARKED "RESUPPLY" IN THE COMMUNICATIONS BUNKER.
HUH. CAN'T BELIEVE I MISSED THAT.
DISCOVERY TEAM. WE LOOK EVERYWHERE.
UH, SAM?
I NEED TO KNOW HOW YOU GOT THIS THING THROUGH THE GRATE.
TELL ME NOW OR MY HEAD WILL EXPLODE.
WELL, FIRST I TOOK THE CLEANING BOT APART.
THEN I PASSED THE PIECES THROUGH.
HUNG THEM WITH STRING AND REASSEMBLED THEM INTO OUR NEW EXPLORATORY ROVER...
...AND WE CONTROL IT WITH THE TABLET? THIS IS GONNA BE GREAT.
CAN WE START NOW?
BEFORE YOU ANSWER, KNOW THAT YOU CAN ONLY ANSWER YES.

DENSITY SCANS TELL US THE MASS IS WILDLY INCONSISTENT. WE'LL HAVE TO BE EXTRA CAREFUL.
INSTEAD OF THE WIDE-BEAM APPROACH WE'D PLANNED FOR, WE'LL SLOWLY CARVE OUT A TRENCH.
IT'LL TAKE LONGER, BUT IT'LL PREVENT A DELUGE.
SO YOU'RE FIRING A LASER INTO A MOUNTAIN OF ICE.
HOW MANY PEOPLE DO YOU NEED?
KAANAN AND I WILL ACT AS SURVEYORS...
...WE'VE GOT GALEN AND RICKERT TO STEADY THE LASER...
...DENIS IS ON CONTROLS, AND NADINE'S OUR STANDBY.
SO, SIX.
YOU ALL CHOSE TO TAKE ON THIS CHALLENGE, BUT YOU CAN'T CHOOSE TO BACK OUT LATER.
MAKE SURE YOU'RE UP FOR IT--AND I DON'T JUST MEAN PHYSICALLY.

BROWNOUT. SOONER THAN PREDICTED...
ICE OR NO ICE, WE LOSE POWER, WE'RE DONE.
YOU DON'T SAY, GALEN.
MIGHT AS WELL HAVE SAID, "DON'T JOSH IT UP".
IT'S NOT LIKE HE'S HERE TO HAVE HIS FEELINGS HURT.
I'M NOT WRONG.
NO. YOU'RE NOT WRONG.
AH. THERE'S THE--
JANN, DID YOU KNOW...?
UH...
YOUR GIRL. ALEA. AND SAM. THEY'VE BEEN, I GUESS, SPENDING TIME TOGETHER.
YEAH. SHE HAD HIM OVER TO THE HOUSE EARLIER.
OH.
SEEMS NICE. ALEA SAYS HE'S PRETTY CLEVER.
I'M SURE HIS FATHER--WELL, BOTH HIS PARENTS--WOULD BE PROUD OF HOW HE TURNED OUT.

I DON'T BELIEVE IT.
WE SHOULD'VE HIT SOMETHING BY NOW, RIGHT?
I MEAN... I DON'T KNOW. WE PASSED THROUGH THAT STRUCTURAL DAMAGE AND NOW I DON'T KNOW WHERE WE ARE.
THE OUTPOST IS SO TINY YOU FORGET JUST HOW BIG THE GENSHIP WAS, I GUESS.
THAT WAS THE LAST OF IT. WE COULD SCAVENGE SOME ROPE, SOME OTHER WIRING...
COULDN'T WE?
THE CAMERA'S POINTED STRAIGHT DOWN.
THERE'S NOTHING THERE. JUST... DARKNESS.
AWW.
AND WE WERE HAVING FUN.
THIS WAS BETTER THAN MY SINGULARITY!
SERIOUSLY...
...THIS IS THE BEST THING SINCE BEFORE STEVEN LEFT.

FSSSSS
NO!
WHY'D YOU LET GO?!
THE ROVER'S GONNA BREAK!
NOT UNTIL IT HITS BOTTOM, SAM!
NOT UNTIL... OH.
THERE YOU GO.

IT'S BEEN LIKE A MIN--
SHH.
WATER! IT HIT WATER!
LIQUID, ANYWAY. COULD BE FUEL--
DIDN'T SEE ANYTHING ELSE...
DAMN, SHORTING OUT. PIXELS...
WISH THERE WAS SOME WAY TO CLEAR IT UP...

WHAT DO YOU SUPPOSE IS THE LAST THING THE LAST LIVING HUMAN WILL EVER SEE?

I DON'T KNOW, BUT GOSH, I SURE WOULD LIKE TO THINK ABOUT *THAT* ALL THE TIME...
HEHH... WELL, *THIS* LIVING HUMAN WOULD HAVE LIKED TO HAVE SEEN NATURAL DAYLIGHT ONCE MORE, AT LEAST.
YOU MAY STILL GET TO.
WE'RE CLOSE TO A SOLUTION TO OUR ICE PROBLEM. MAYBE THEN WE CAN DISPLAY THE FROST AGAIN.
YES, MAYBE SO.
KAREN...

...WHEN YOU CARE FOR PEOPLE'S HEALTH AS A VOCATION, IT DOESN'T NECESSARILY MEAN YOU CARE *ABOUT* THEM.
BUT SOME, YOU CONNECT WITH.
A FEW BECOME LIKE FAMILY.
YOU ARE FAMILY.

TELL HIM.
TELL SAM THAT YOU WERE ONCE IN LOVE WITH HIS FATHER.

EXPLAIN HOW IT WAS BEFORE SAM'S MOTHER. THAT HE WAS FAITHFUL.
IT'LL BE DIFFICULT AT FIRST, BUT HE WILL APPRECIATE IT. HE'LL COME TO SEE YOU IN A DIFFERENT LIGHT.
AND WHEN HE ASKS WHY WE DIDN'T STAY TOGETHER? I'M SUPPOSED TO TELL HIM WHAT?

YOU COULD SAY IT DOESN'T MATTER. THAT YOUR BREAK-UP MADE HIS EXISTENCE POSSIBLE.
YOU COULD TELL HIM WHAT YOU TOLD HIS FATHER--THAT YOU WERE INFERTILE, THAT HE NEEDED TO FIND SOMEONE TO REPRODUCE WITH.

OR I COULD TELL HIM I WAS SELFISH AND AFRAID. THAT I PUT MYSELF BEFORE OUR SPECIES' SURVIVAL.
THAT I MADE YOU COMPLICIT IN A LIE--NOT JUST TO HIS FATHER, BUT TO THE ENTIRE OUTPOST.
BECAUSE I DIDN'T WANT A CHILD.

THAT PART IS A SECRET THAT CAN LEAVE WITH ME.
IF YOU'D LIKE IT TO.

FORGET WHAT I SAID ABOUT THE SKY.
I COULD NEVER TIRE OF OUR OWN SUNSETS.

--HAVE THE LATEST VIDCLIP COMPILATION READY--
NO, YOU CAN STOP MAKING THOSE. SAM'S NOT A SECURITY RISK.
SURE THING, CHIEF. YOUR SYSTEM SCAN'S ALMOST DONE.
THANKS.
SAM? IS THAT YOU?

SAM? GOOD.
I'D LIKE YOU TO TAKE A SEAT SO--
SAM, THERE'S SOMETHING I HAVE TO--
SAM?
SAM...!
OH. WELL, HEY.
SO GLAD WE HAD THIS TALK.

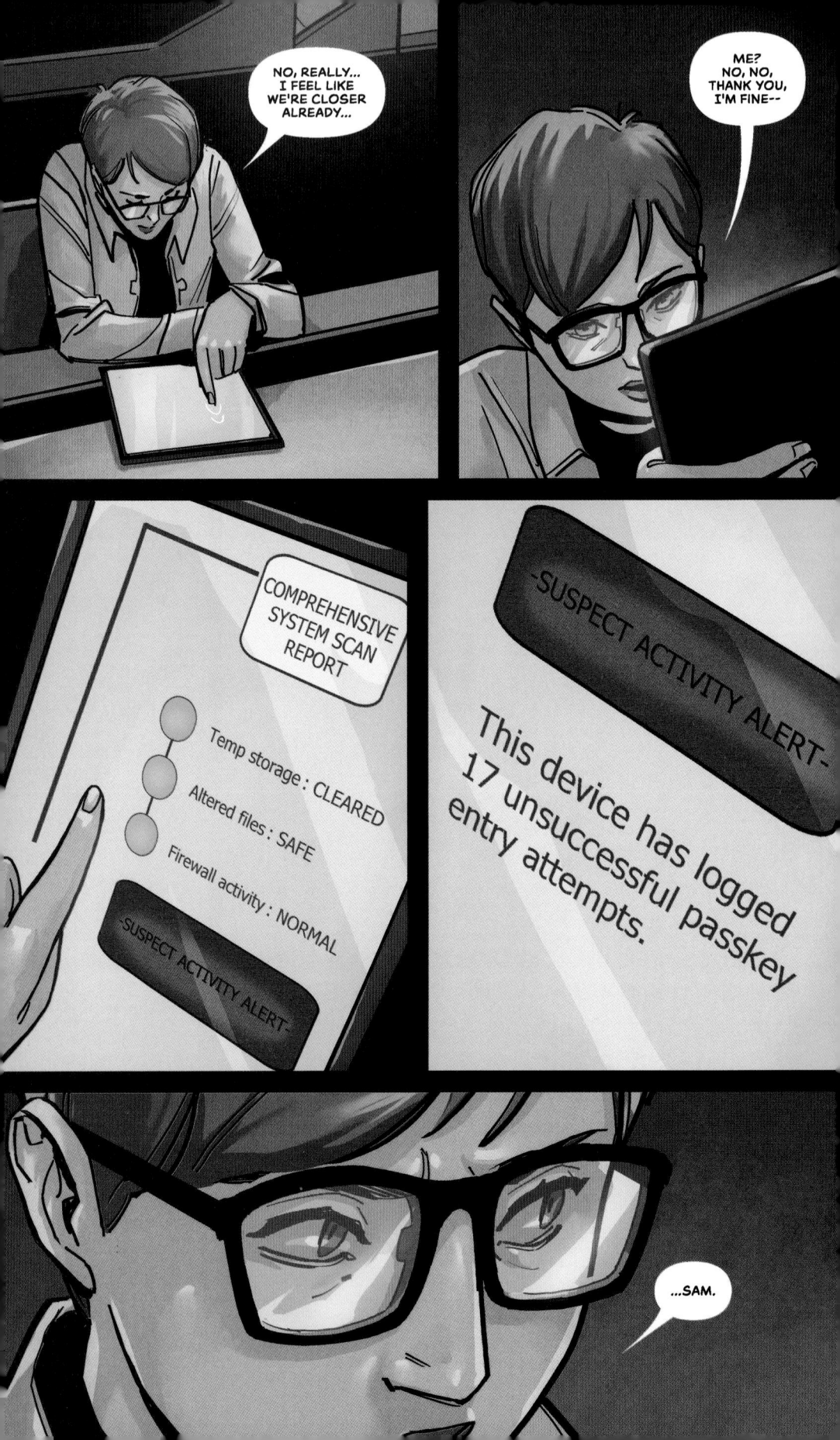
NO, REALLY... I FEEL LIKE WE'RE CLOSER ALREADY...
ME? NO, NO, THANK YOU, I'M FINE--
COMPREHENSIVE SYSTEM SCAN REPORT
Temp storage : CLEARED
Altered files : SAFE
Firewall activity : NORMAL
-SUSPECT ACTIVITY ALERT-
-SUSPECT ACTIVITY ALERT-
This device has logged 17 unsuccessful passkey entry attempts.
...SAM.

ALL SET, DENIS.
KAANAN?
GREEN LIGHT HERE.
HOW'S OUR STANDBY?
STANDBY IS WISHING SHE HAD SOMETHING TO DO.
LET'S GET THIS FINISHED.
YES. LET'S.
I SUPPOSE I *COULD* STAND CLEAR OF THE GIANT LASER BEFORE I FIRE IT UP...
THAT SEEMS INTELLIGENT.
AND--

WWWWHMMM
KRAK
BAM
NHH!
WWHMMM
TOO STRONG!

KAANAN! NOT THAT WAY, YOU'LL BE CRUSHED!
CRAC
SKAAAAA
DENIS! SHUT IT DOWN!
DENIS?
HNN!
I GOT IT!

THE CALIBRATIONS ARE OFF! I TOLD FABRICATION TEAM TO--
STOP ALREADY, KAANAN.
YOU CAN COVER YOUR ASS LATER.
THERE. IT'S OFF.
TAP
I'M NOT COVERING MY-- I'M ANALYZING THE SITUATION.
WE'RE GOING TO NEED TO FIX THE--
POC
DAMN IT--

KAANAN?! TALK TO US!
OH NO.
KAANAN!
I CAN'T.
I CAN'T.
I CAN'T.
I CAAAN'T!
KAANAN, GET UP NOW OR ELSE--

BROOOOM
KAANAN!
SWOOSH
FFFWOOSH

IT TOOK FIVE DAYS, BUT THEY EVENTUALLY VAPORIZED THE WATER AND GOT BACK IN THROUGH THE AIRLOCK.
CAN'T STOP THINKING ABOUT WHAT IT WOULD HAVE BEEN LIKE, BEING ONE OF THEM.
BEING KAANAN.

THERE'S A DIFFERENCE, ISN'T THERE?
THE ABSTRACT IDEA OF DYING IN THE FROST, VERSUS CONFRONTING THE REALITY OF IT.
YOU KNOW WHAT THAT'S LIKE. I DO, A LITTLE.

KAANAN DROWNED IN ICE WATER, AND I THOUGHT, "GLAD IT WASN'T ME".
SAME AS AFTER WATCHING YOU WALK OUT THERE.
THING IS, STEVEN...

TURNS OUT I DON'T WANT TO DIE.
BUT WHY DO I STILL *FEEL* LIKE I DO?

FEEL LIKE WHAT?

SORRY. THAT'S NOSY. I'M BEING NOSY.
YOU'RE UP LATE.
I HAVEN'T SLEPT MUCH LATELY, AFTER WHAT WE SAW.

WE DON'T KNOW WHAT WE SAW.
IT WAS ALIVE, SAM. IT WAS... AWFUL.

HAVE YOU SAID ANYTHING TO ANYONE?
YOU AND ALEA SAID NOT TO. SO, NO.

THEY PUT STEVEN'S PORTRAIT AWAY.
IT'S KAANAN'S TURN TO BE MOURNED NOW. THERE'S USUALLY LESS TIME ON DISPLAY THAN HE HAD BECAUSE OF--
COPYCATS. YEAH.

I SHOULD SLEEP.
SAM?

I TOLD ALEA, NOW I'M TELLING YOU...
DON'T GO DOWN THERE. WHATEVER THAT IS BENEATH US...

...IT'S DEATH.

I'VE BEEN SLOWLY GOING INSANE.
MY PARENTS WERE OUT THERE AND I COULDN'T DO ANYTHING-- COULDN'T HELP.
AND WHAT WE SAW-- CAN'T DO ANYTHING ABOUT THAT CAUSE MY HEAD'S NOT ON STRAIGHT AND PEOPLE ARE CHECKING ON ME AND ELLA NIGHT AND DAY...
AND WHERE'VE YOU BEEN? HIDING FROM ME? I WANNA FIND MORE WIRE SPOOLS. TAKE ANOTHER LOOK.
Y'KNOW, ALEA...I DON'T...
WHAT, ARE YOU LYSS NOW? ARE YOU FREAKED OUT?
WE DISCOVERED LIFE, SAM. LIFE.

YOU DON'T ***KNOW*** THAT.
ONLY BECAUSE ***YOU BROKE--***

ONLY BECAUSE YOU BROKE THE TABLET AND WE LOST THE RECORDING.
BUT IF WE REPEAT THE EXPERIMENT, WE CAN CONFIRM. IT'S SIMPLE.

I DON'T KNOW. KAREN'S CLAMPING DOWN ON ME FOR SOME REASON.
SHE'S EVEN CHECKED OUT MY ROOM.

THE PROJECTOR?
I MADE A BETTER HIDING SPOT. AFTER IT WAS ***STOLEN*** FROM ME.

PLEASE, SAM. WE'LL BE MORE CAUTIOUS, TAKE OUR TIME...
EVEN IF YOU DON'T BUY WHAT STEVEN SAID, YOU'RE ***CURIOUS.***

WELL, IT'S NOT THAT I--
I MEAN, I DUNNO. MAYBE...

MAYBE WE SHOULD JUST GET BACK TO OUR LIVES.

WHEN ARE YOU GOING BACK OUT?
SECURITY TEAM IS MEETING WITH US TOMORROW, ELLA. WE HAVE A PLAN, BUT THEY HAVE TO APPROVE IT.
OR YOU COULD JUST NOT DO ANY OF THAT AND COMPLETELY GIVE UP.

ALEA.
WHY NOT? IT'S THE OUTPOST WAY, ISN'T IT?

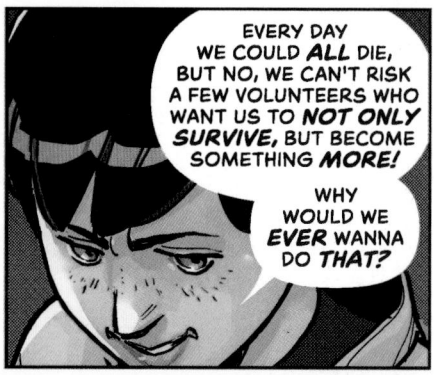
EVERY DAY WE COULD ALL DIE, BUT NO, WE CAN'T RISK A FEW VOLUNTEERS WHO WANT US TO NOT ONLY SURVIVE, BUT BECOME SOMETHING MORE!
WHY WOULD WE EVER WANNA DO THAT?

NOW LOOK WHAT YOU DID, ALEA.

clic

YOU KNOW, KAANAN THOUGHT HE ALMOST HAD THESE POWER FLUCTUATIONS FIGURED OUT.
I DON'T SUPPOSE ANYONE ELSE IN PLANNING TEAM HAS THE BRAIN TO TACKLE HIS DATA.
NOT TO SPEAK ILL, BUT HE WAS KIND OF OFF-BASE.

DID HE TELL YOU HIS THEORY?
HE SAID THE ICE STORM AND BROWNOUTS WERE A TOTAL *COINCIDENCE.*
THAT THE *DATA* SUPPORTED AN ELECTROMAGNETIC *ANOMALY* THAT'S BEEN GROWING FOR *YEARS...*
clic

HEY. LIGHT'S ON.
WHERE ARE YOU GOING?
NEED TO CHECK ON SOMETHING.

THE POWER WASN'T *REALLY* HER FAULT, DAD.

OH, ELLA. A PERFECTLY RANDOM OPPORTUNITY TO BLAME SOMETHING ON YOUR SISTER AND YOU TURN IT DOWN?

I DON'T EVEN KNOW YOU ANYMORE.

YOU'RE NEVER FUNNY.

...I DON'T KNOW HOW OR WHY, BUT THIS IS WHAT I AM NOW.
I CAN'T GO BACK.
...I DON'T KNOW HOW OR WHY, BUT THIS IS WHAT I AM NOW.
ARE YOU AWAKE?
I KNOW I'VE BEEN... WORSE LATELY. QUIET.
WHATEVER IT IS, YOU CAN TELL ME.

SOMETIMES I WISH...I COULD FIND THE REST OF US. GO TO OTHER WORLDS.
WHEN I THINK ABOUT HOW I DON'T GET TO EXPERIENCE ANY OF IT. THAT I'M... HERE...
IT HURTS.
YOU'VE ALWAYS BEEN INQUISITIVE. YOU SEE MORE THAN MOST PEOPLE.
ALL THAT IS WHAT GOT ME WANDERING FROM MY FAMILY WHEN THE CELL CAME.
YOU COULDN'T HAVE SAVED THEM.
YEAH, BUT SOMETIMES I THINK MAYBE I WAS...
I JUST WANT...
WHY CAN'T I JUST BE NORMAL?
SAM...
DON'T YOU EVER BE THAT.
DON'T YOU DARE.

I HEAR WHAT YOU'RE TELLING ME...

...AND IT ALL SOUNDS LOGICAL AND VERY SCIENTIFIC, BUT I HAVE A DUTY TO REMIND YOU THAT SCIENCE IS HARDLY AN EXACT SCIENCE FOR US.
THAT'S NOT ENTIRELY FAIR--

NO?
DIDN'T WE JUST PROVE OUT THERE THAT, WHEN IT COMES TO UNDERSTANDING OUR ANCESTORS' TECH, WE'RE A BUNCH OF NOVICES?

KAANAN HAD THE FIGURES RIGHT. THEY WEREN'T PROPERLY TRANSPOSED--
IT WAS A BAD CALIBRATION. THAT'S ALL.
THAT KILLED ONE OF OUR BRIGHTEST MINDS, AND ALMOST GOT GALEN'S SKULL CRACKED OPEN.
NONE OF US WANT ANYONE TO DIE, KAREN...

...BUT WE CAN'T SIT HERE AND LET ALL OF US DIE BECAUSE WE'RE AFRAID TO RISK A FEW VOLUNTEERS WHO WANT TO DO SOMETHING ABOUT IT.

OKAY, KAANAN...
LET'S LOOK AT THOSE DATA CHARTS OF YOURS AGAIN.

I FEEL LIKE I NEED TO KEEP REPEATING MYSELF TO YOU...
MY JOB IS TO ***SECURE*** THE OUTPOST. EVERY TIME WE OPEN THAT AIRLOCK, WE PLACE ***EVERYONE*** IN DANGER.

IT'S AN ***AIRLOCK,*** KAREN. IT'S ***DESIGNED*** TO BE ***SAFE.***
DESIGNED BY EXPERTS ***WE*** CAN'T CONSULT WITH TO ENSURE IT ***REMAINS*** SAFE.
I'M SAYING WE HAVE TO BE ***CAUTIOUS.***

I THANK YOU FOR WHAT YOU'RE ALL DOING. REALLY, I DO...

...BUT WE'RE GOING OVER THE PLAN AGAIN AND AGAIN UNTIL I'M ***SURE*** YOUR NEXT TRIP OUTSIDE ACTUALLY ***FIXES*** THINGS.

ANOTHER THING--SALVAGE MORE CAMS. WE NEED FEWER BLIND SPOTS.
WHY? WE GOT A PROBLEM?
ASSUME WE'VE ALWAYS GOT A PROBLEM.

KNOCK KNOCK
SHE'S HOME. SHE'LL HEAR.
I JUST HAVE A QUESTION.
WHEN ALL IS SAID AND DONE, WHEN IT'S ALL OVER...
WOULD YOU WANT TO SAY YOU LIVED YOUR LIFE WAITING TO DIE?
OR WOULD YOU WANT TO SAY SOMETHING DIFFERENT?
STAK

I COULD STAND HERE ALL NIGHT, EVERY NIGHT.
BUT YOU'RE SAYING YOU JUMPED FROM HERE, AND SURVIVED BECAUSE OF THE GRAVSYNC.
EXCEPT YOU GOT HURT BECAUSE YOUR CALCULATIONS WERE OFF, BECAUSE OF AN ANOMALY THAT'S CAUSING THE BROWNOUTS.
PRETTY MUCH. AND HERE'S THE LAST BIT.
I KNOW WHERE THE ANOMALY IS.
INSIDE THE SCRAP WAREHOUSE.
BUT I NEVER SAW... WHAT COULD IT BE?
YOU WANNA KNOW. YOU HAVE TO KNOW.
I DON'T HAVE ACCESS ANYMORE.
YEAH, BUT LOOK.
HERE'S WHAT I'M THINKING, AND IT SOUNDS COMPLETELY CRAZY, BUT HEAR ME OUT...
RUN AND JUMP.

WELL, YEAH, EXACTLY.
AND LOOK, I'M NOT ASKING YOU TO DO ANYTHING YOU DON'T WANT, BUT I'M TELLING YOU THE MATH IS SOLID, AND I THINK--
SAM?
KAP
LET'S GO!

SAM...
SWISH

BAM
AAH!
HFF...
THUMP!
STUPID.
THAT WAS COMPLETELY...

NO! SAM--
GOT YOU, I GOT YOU--

GOOD JOB.

THE ADRENALINE...!
I CAN'T--DID YOU SEE HOW I--? AND THE WAY YOU-- I MEAN--IT WAS JUST--
THAT WAS BETTER THAN MY FREEFALL.
I WANNA DO THAT AGAIN.
EXCEPT THE LAST PART.

LYSS WOULD LOVE THAT. FORGET THOSE SKATES...
ALEA.
YOU SEE IT, RIGHT?

KRAK
THAT'S IT. IT'S GOTTA BE.
THE SOURCE OF THE ENERGY FLUCTUATIONS.
THE CAUSE OF THE BROWN-OUTS. THE REASON THE GRAVSYNC'S WONKIER THAN IT SHOULD BE.
WHO KNOWS WHAT ELSE?
HOW DID I NEVER SEE IT BEFORE...?
IT'S ONLY OBVIOUS FROM ABOVE.
YOU NEEDED A DIFFERENT PERSPECTIVE.

I DID ALWAYS WONDER WHY IT WAS KINDA CHILLY IN HERE.
YEAH. THAT BREEZE...
YOU DON'T THINK IT'S THE FROST...?
NO. IT WOULD BE WAY WORSE.
SO IT'S THIS ANOMALY OF YOURS?
IT HAS TO BE.
CAN'T EVEN SEE ANYTHING...
CAREFUL!
THERE. WE CAN SEE A LITTLE BETTER NOW.
IS THAT...?
IT IS.

THAT'S IT.
WE'LL BE SAFE.
UNTIL THE NEXT CATASTROPHE.

THE SUN WILL MELT THE REST OF THE MOUNTAIN OFF THE DOME, BUT WHAT ABOUT THE REMAINDER?
RUNOFF WILL MELT IT, NADINE. LIKE A LESS DRAMATIC VERSION OF WHAT HAPPENED IN HERE.
IF NOT, WE'LL MAKE CLEARING ALL OF THAT PART OF OUR NEXT EXPEDITION.
DENIS? WHAT IS IT?
DON'T TELL ME IT'S HULL DAMAGE.
JUST A SERENDIPITOUS ACT OF CHAOS.
NO...

ENGINEERING TEAM SAYS THERE'S ALREADY A SIGNIFICANT REDUCTION IN DOME PRESSURE.
IT'S NOT OVER, BUT AS LONG AS WE'RE MONITORING, THERE SHOULDN'T BE SURPRISES.
THANK YOU.
IF THAT'S ALL, CHIEF, THEN WE'LL START PLOTTING OUR NEXT EXCURSION. THERE'S REASON TO BELIEVE OUR LAST TRIP MIGHT HAVE--
DENIS.
JANN.
THIS CELL DIDN'T HURT US AS BADLY AS THE LAST, BUT IT WAS ALMOST THE END OF US.
OUR PRIORITY NOW IS MAKING US SAFER WHEN THE NEXT CELL HITS. AND WITH KAANAN GONE...
WE'RE STILL ON PLANNING TEAM DUTY, YOU MEAN. WAS THIS A COUNCIL DECISION?
IT'S NOT THE ONLY DECISION THE COUNCIL MADE.

I'M SORRY, ALEA.
IT WAS INEVITABLE, RIGHT? EVERYONE QUESTIONED THE NEED FOR DISCOVERY TEAM. EVEN YOU, MITCHELL, STEVEN...
NOW IT DOESN'T HAVE TO BE QUESTIONED ANYMORE, I GUESS.
DISCOVERY TEAM IS GONE.
DOES THAT MEAN...? ARE YOU DONE, TOO? EXPLORING WITH SAM?
THE STUFF WE'RE DOING, IT'S... A PASTIME, LYSS.
CURIOSITY.
NO ONE'S GETTING HURT.
SO YOU'RE SAYING THAT THING WE SAW ISN'T DANGEROUS? OR ARE YOU LIKE SAM NOW, DENYING WE EVEN SAW ANYTHING?
THAT'S NOT WHAT HE'S--
SAM'S... CAREFUL. THAT'S ALL.
I CAN'T IGNORE WHAT'S OUT THERE.
I PROMISE, WHATEVER WE DO, WE'LL BE SAFE.
BUT I HAVE TO KEEP LOOKING. I HAVE TO.
YOU CAN JOIN US AGAIN IF YOU CHANGE YOUR MIND.
I WON'T SAY IT WASN'T FUN FOR A WHILE...

HAVE YOU SPOKEN TO MITCHELL?
NOT SINCE BEFORE HIS FIGHT. HARDLY KNOW WHERE I'D EVEN FIND HIM ANYMORE. CERTAINLY NOT HERE.
PRETTY SOON WE WON'T BE HERE ANYMORE, EITHER. FULL-TIME INTERNS...
YEAH...
HONESTLY, IF IT WASN'T FOR BEING FRIENDS WITH HIS SISTER, IF IT WASN'T FOR STEVEN...
WOULD SOMEONE LIKE MITCHELL EVEN BE MY FRIEND?
BUT HE IS YOUR FRIEND.
I KNOW HE SHOWS IT IN WEIRD WAYS, BUT SO DO I SOMETIMES.
YOU'VE GOT A POINT. I'M STUCK WITH BOTH OF YOU, AREN'T I?
PEOPLE KEEP SAYING THINGS ARE GONNA GET BACK TO NORMAL NOW.
THAT'D BE NICE, WOULDN'T IT? IT'LL NEVER BE THE WAY IT WAS, BUT IT COULD BE CLOSE.
ANYWAY...
I HOPE THEY'RE RIGHT.

I'VE...BEEN TRYING TO HACK YOUR PERSONAL TABLET. I WANTED ACCESS TO THE WAREHOUSE. SO I COULD MAKE STUFF.
I'M SORRY.

SO THERE'S THAT. AND THE AIRLOCK.
SEEMS TO BE A PATTERN WITH YOU.
I WANT TO TRUST YOU, SAM. SECURITY TEAM IS TOO IMPORTANT FOR THAT TRUST TO BE UNCONDITIONAL.
BUT YOU CONFESSED PROACTIVELY TO ONE OF YOUR WRONGS.
AND THAT'S SOMETHING, SO...

PROVISIONAL INTERNSHIP. WELCOME BACK.
BUT IF YOU WERE ANYBODY ELSE, YOU'D BE OUT, UNDERSTAND ME? NO MORE TROUBLE.

YES, CHIEF. THANK YOU.

CODE RETRIEVAL
WAREHOUS _
DELETING
SEC-CAM PROFILE
08SEC1184x109
08SEC1184x110
08SEC1184x118
08SEC1184x121
...

WAIT...
WAIT...
OKAY.
HEY, CHIEF...
ANOTHER BROWNOUT?
POWER'S ON OVER THERE.
TRY ANOTHER CAM IN THE AREA.
TAP TAP

NOPE. WHOLE ZONE'S OUT.
WHERE?
NEAR THE AIRLOCK.
SO THIS IS IT...
TIME'S ALMOST UP. COME ON.
EVERYONE STOP AND CHECK THE LOGS.
FOR WHAT?
ANYTHING.
CHIEF! IT'S BACK ON.
PROBABLY A FAULTY NODE.
CHECK IT. THEN CHECK AGAIN.
RIGHT AWAY.
KEEP AUDITING THOSE LOGS. I WANT TO KNOW EXACTLY WHAT HAPPENED.

NNH.
YOUR DAD'S GOT NARROW SHOULDERS.
MINE DOESN'T REALLY FIT EITHER.
ARE YOU SEALED IN?
I'M GOOD. YOU?
ALL SET.
WE'RE REALLY DOING THIS...
FEEL LIKE TURNING BACK?
YES.
BUT NO.

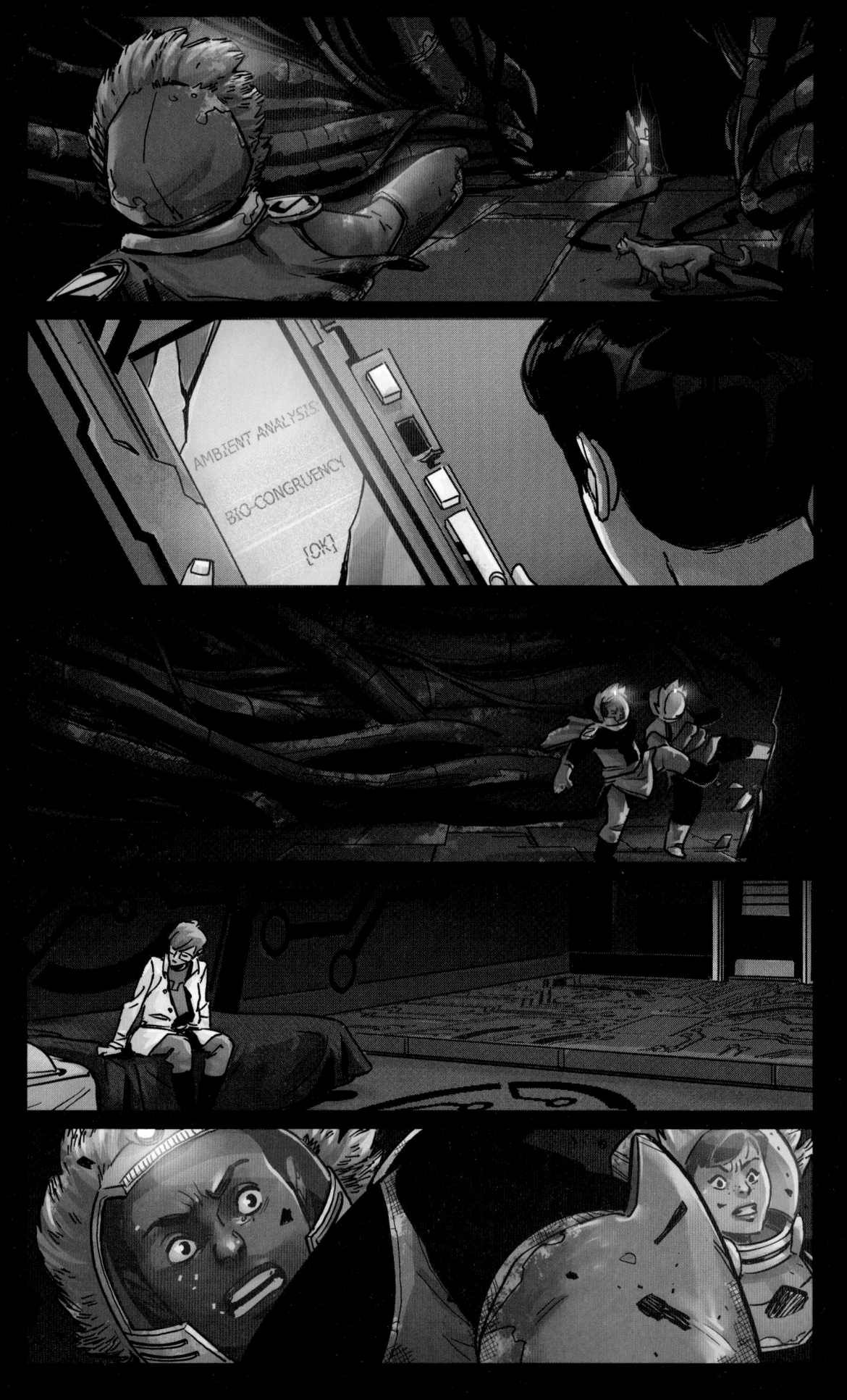
AMBIENT ANALYSIS:
BIO-CONGRUENCY
[OK]

I'M THROUGH.
THIS IS WHERE THE CATS GO? HOW COLD IS IT?
DUNNO, BUT DEFINITELY COLD. YOU CAN SEE IT.
SHOULD'VE BROUGHT A TABLET--
HELLO.
THIS ENCOUNTER IS UNEXPECTED.

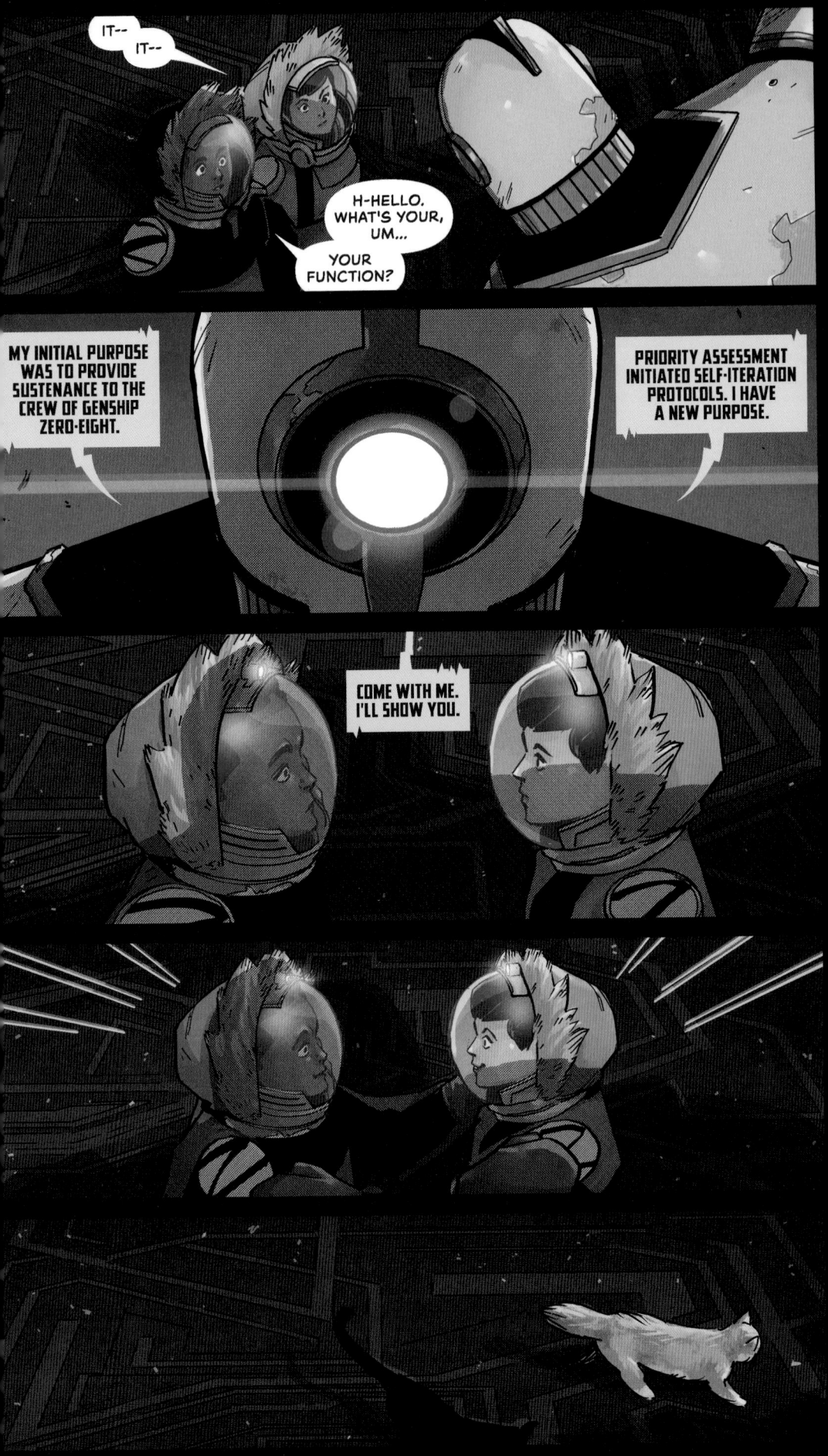
IT--
IT--
H-HELLO. WHAT'S YOUR, UM...
YOUR FUNCTION?
MY INITIAL PURPOSE WAS TO PROVIDE SUSTENANCE TO THE CREW OF GENSHIP ZERO-EIGHT.
PRIORITY ASSESSMENT INITIATED SELF-ITERATION PROTOCOLS. I HAVE A NEW PURPOSE.
COME WITH ME. I'LL SHOW YOU.

to be
continued

we bury us,
we bury
everyone.

GENSHIP

MAX POP. 1 MILLION

BIOME

A. DOWNTOWN
B. INDUSTRIAL QUADRANT
C. FARMING QUADRANT
D. HOUSING QUAD. ALPHA
E. HOUSING QUAD. BETA
F. LIGHT VEHICLE AIRLOCK

STEM COUPLING

G. GRAV-SYNC ENGINES
H. CREW QUARTERS
I. DOCKING PORT

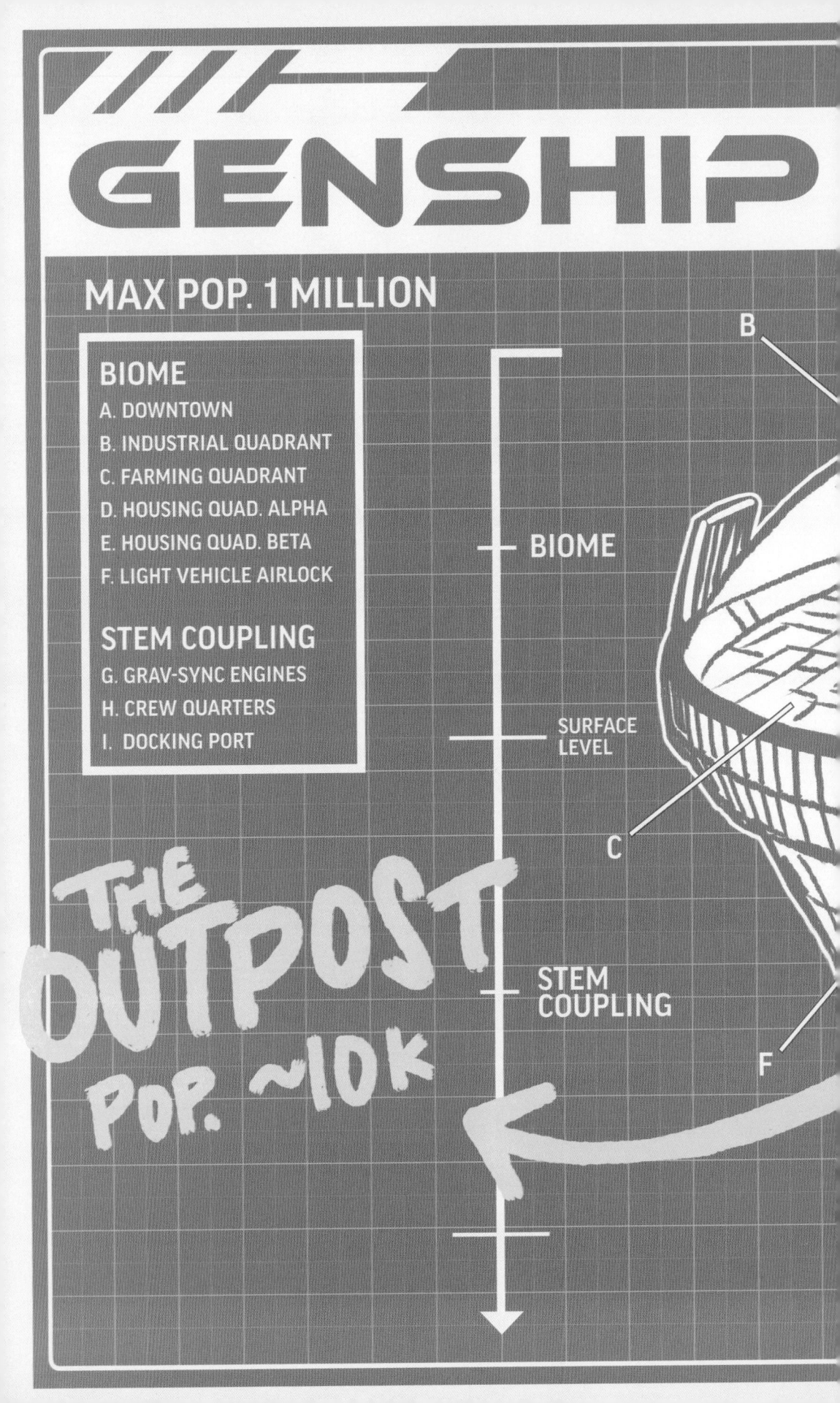

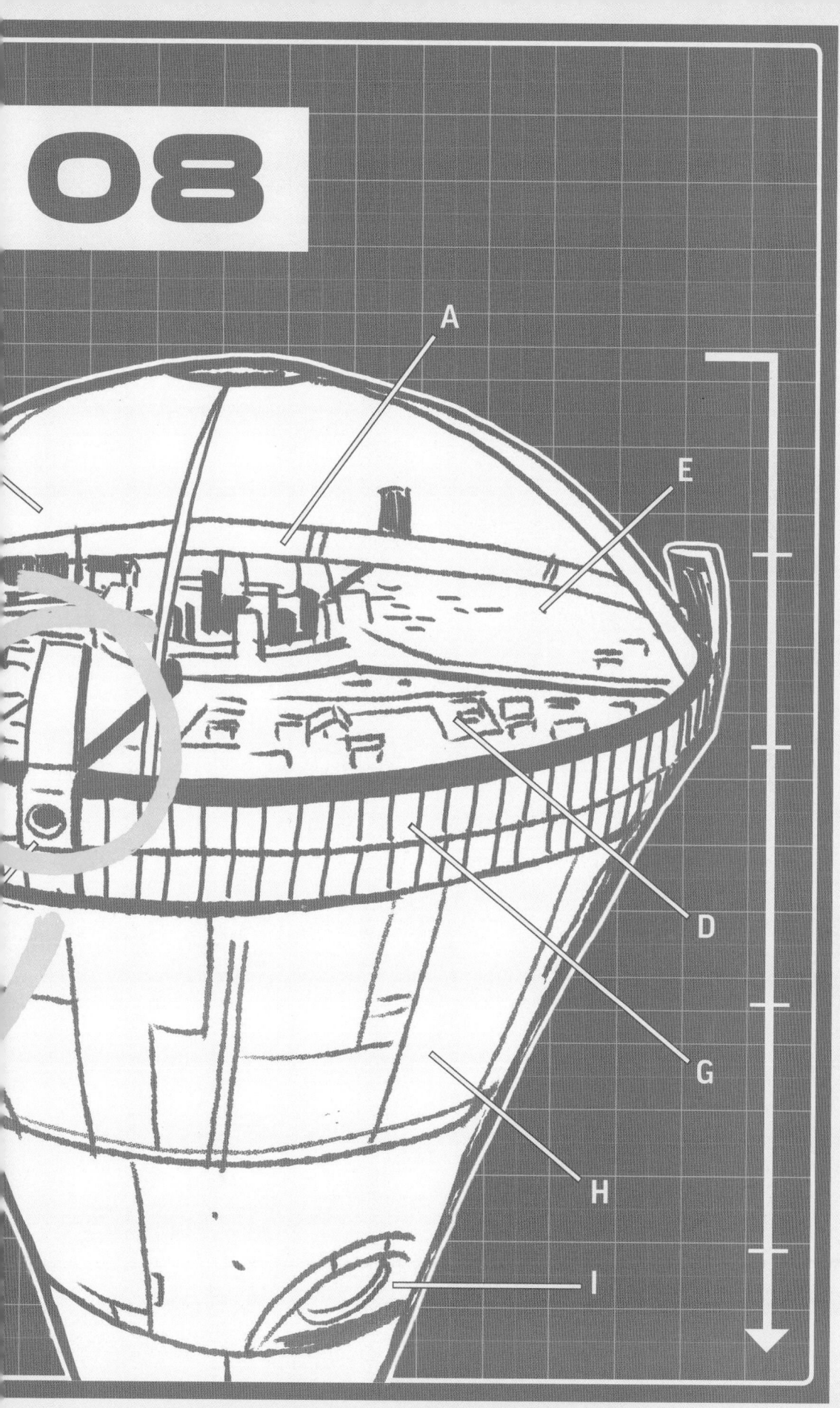
A
E
D
G
H
I

For more tales from ROBERT KIRKMAN and SKYBOUND

VOL. 1: EACH OTHER'S THROATS
ISBN: 978-1-5343-1210-4
$16.99

CHAPTER ONE
ISBN: 978-1-5343-0642-4
$9.99

CHAPTER TWO
ISBN: 978-1-5343-1057-5
$16.99

VOL. 1: HOMECOMING TP
ISBN: 978-1-63215-231-2
$9.99

VOL. 2: CALL TO ADVENTURE TP
ISBN: 978-1-63215-446-0
$12.99

VOL. 3: ALLIES AND ENEMIES TP
ISBN: 978-1-63215-683-9
$12.99

VOL. 4: FAMILY HISTORY TP
ISBN: 978-1-63215-871-0
$12.99

VOL. 5: BELLY OF THE BEAST TP
ISBN: 978-1-5343-0218-1
$12.99

VOL. 6: FATHERHOOD TP
ISBN: 978-1-53430-498-7
$14.99

VOL. 7: BLOOD BROTHERS TP
ISBN: 978-1-5343-1053-7
$14.99

VOL. 1: DEEP IN THE HEART TP
ISBN: 978-1-5343-0331-7
$16.99

VOL. 2: THE EYES UPON YOU TP
ISBN: 978-1-5343-0665-3
$16.99

VOL. 3: LONGHORNS TP
ISBN: 978-1-5343-1050-6
$16.99

VOL. 1: ARTIST TP
ISBN: 978-1-5343-0242-6
$16.99

VOL. 2: WARRIOR TP
ISBN: 978-1-5343-0506-9
$16.99

VOL. 1
ISBN: 978-1-60706-420-6
$9.99

VOL. 2
ISBN: 978-1-60706-568-5
$14.99

VOL. 3
ISBN: 978-1-60706-667-5
$12.99

VOL. 4
ISBN: 978-1-60706-843-3
$12.99

BIRTHRIGHT™, EXTREMITY™ , OUTER DARKNESS™, and REDNECK™ © 2019 Skybound, LLC. SUPER DINOSAUR™ © 2019 Robert Kirkman, LLC. OBLIVION SONG™ © 2019 Robert Kirkman, LLC and Lorenzo De Felici.
Image Comics® and its logos are registered trademarks of Image Comics, Inc. Skybound and its logos are © and ™ of Skybound, LLC. All rights reserved.